My First Time

The New Baby

Kate Petty, Lisa Kopper, and Jim Pipe

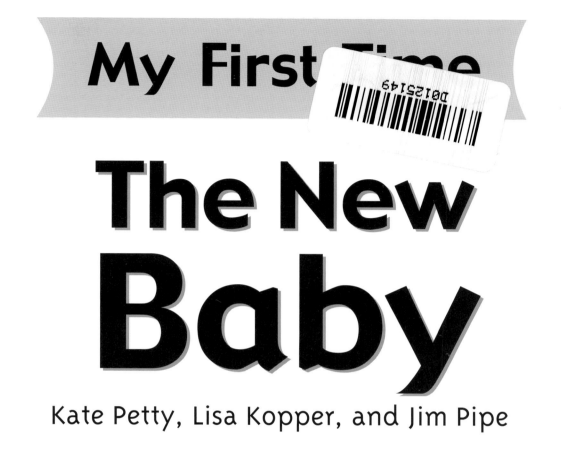

Stargazer Books
Mankato, Minnesota

© Aladdin Books Ltd 2009

Designed and produced by
Aladdin Books Ltd

*First published in 2009
in the United States by*
Stargazer Books,
distributed by Black Rabbit Books
PO Box 3263, Mankato, MN 56002

Printed in the United States   All rights reserved

Illustrator: Lisa Kopper   Photocredits: All photos from istockphoto.com.

Library of Congress Cataloging-in-Publication Data

Petty, Kate.
  The new baby / Kate Petty.
     p. cm. -- (My first time)
  Summary: Sam's household gets a lot of excitement when his mother goes to the hospital and comes
home with a new baby sister for him.
  Includes index.
  ISBN 978-1-59604-175-2
  [1. Babies--Fiction. 2. Brothers and sisters--Fiction.] I. Title.
  PZ7.P44814Ne 2009
  E--dc22
                          2008015282

About this book

New experiences can be scary for young children. This series will help them to understand situations they may find themselves in, by explaining in a friendly way what can happen.

This book can be used as a starting point for discussing issues. The questions in some of the boxes ask children about their own experiences.

The stories will also help children to master basic reading skills and learn new vocabulary.

It can help if you read the first sentence to children, and then encourage them to read the rest of the page or story. At the end, try looking through the book again to find where the words in the glossary are used.

Contents

Sam's Mom has got a very big stomach.
Sam can't sit on her lap now.

"Never mind," says Mom,
"I won't be like this for much longer."

Sam leans against Mom instead and they make themselves comfortable.

He feels the baby kicking inside her. Perhaps the baby enjoys stories too!

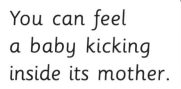

You can feel a baby kicking inside its mother.

5

Mom gets things ready for the baby.
"Was I ever this little?" asks Sam.

"Yes," says Mom, "I'll find some photos
of you when you were tiny."

Sam laughs. "Wasn't I funny?"

"Little babies are often funny," says Mom.
"I expect this baby will make you
laugh sometimes."

Dad is taking Mom to the hospital
because the baby is ready to be born.

Dad calls Sam's friends and they come
to take him to the park.

When Sam gets home, Grandma is there to give him his supper.

Grandma lets him skip his bath tonight and doesn't mind if he stays up late!

Would you like a new brother or sister?

"Wake up, Sam!" Dad hasn't slept at all.

"You've got a baby sister!" says Dad.
"We think we'll call her Jenny.
How do you like that name?"

They stop for presents on the way
to the hospital. "Hurry up, Sam,
Mom's waiting." Sam chooses a panda
for the baby and some flowers for Mom.

At the hospital they go up in an elevator.

Sam can hear the newborn babies as soon as the doors open.

Newborn babies can make a lot of noise!

"Where's the baby?" She's just waking up.

Sam gazes at his tiny new sister.
She's very small and rather wrinkled.
"Hello, Jenny," says Sam.

Today they bring Mom and Jenny home.
Sam is glad to have Mom back.
He's looking forward
to showing Jenny his things.

14

But Jenny goes straight to bed.
So does Mom! Dad is busy
so Sam helps himself to a drink. Oops!

Dad decides it's time for a cuddle.

You can help at bathtime.

Jenny keeps Mom and Dad very busy.
She needs to be bathed...
and changed... and fed...
and changed again.

Sometimes they wish
she'd go to sleep.

16

Jenny has lots of visitors.
She has lots of presents too.
The rattle doesn't stop her crying.
But presents always cheer Sam up!

Jenny is dressed to go out today.
Sam and Dad are taking her for a walk.

Be careful with the carriage!
It's hard work getting it down the steps.

18

The neighbors stop to look at the baby.
Sam feels quite proud of her.

Sam pushes the carriage.
Jenny falls asleep.
Well done, Sam.

It's fun to push a baby carriage or stroller.

Sam talks to Jenny as Dad changes her diaper.
She watches him all the time.

Sam laughs at the funny faces she makes.
It's her bedtime at last.

"Come and sit on my lap, Sam," says Mom.

Mom reads Sam a bedtime story.
Sam can't imagine life without Jenny, but
sometimes it's nice to have Mom all to himself.

cuddle

Mom
and
baby

crying

rattle

carrier

baby lotion

reading
a story

diaper

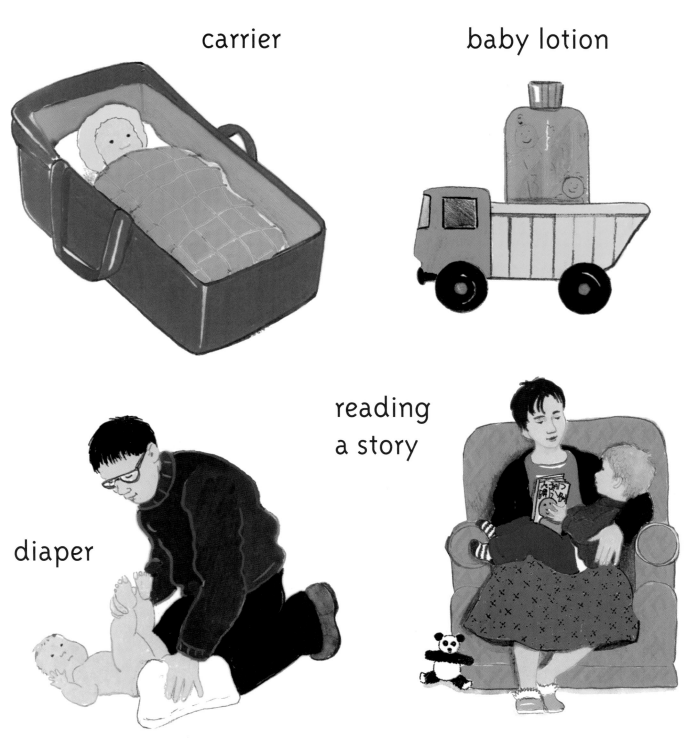

Index

Find out more

Find out more about a new baby in the family at:

www.kidshealth.org
www.childcareaware.org
www.parenthood.com
www.parentstalk.com